LANDCASTER PRESS

Far Louder Than Goliath

(or *Indignation*)

Thomas G. Jewusiak

Far Louder Than Goliath

(or *Indignation*)

Jacket Design by Thomas G. Jewusiak

Cover Painting by Thomas G. Jewusiak

Printed by Hand on the Outer Banks

Crucifixion, Paul Tripp, Petersen, John Marks and *Jackie Gleason* were published previously in a work entitled *The Great Landzman* (©2015) of which they form an indissoluble and essential part. They are reprinted here with the permission of the publisher, Landscaster Press.

"*Far Louder Than Goliath*" was published previously under the title "*Far Louder Than Goliath Would*" in *Stone Country* a literary magazine (77:1 F 77 p. 10) under the nom de plume Thomas M. Gregory

Olaf (upon what were once knees)

      does almost ceaselessly repeat

           "there is some shit I will not eat"

From E. E. Cummings

        i sing of Olaf glad and big

First Paperback Edition

3rd Printing

Jewusiak, Thomas G.

Far Louder Than Goliath

(or Indignation)

ISBN-10:0-9970967-5-6

ISBN-13:978-0-9970967-5-0

Some of these poems and stories were written in old growth ancient virgin forests. While the author was living in the woods, he hurt no old trees in any way.

LANDCASTER PRESS
West Palm Beach
LandcasterPress.com
LandcasterPress@aol.com

The Temptation

Take your pact of blood back from the table.

Take back the razor.

(Your panegyrics are pathetic.)

Take back the names broken down alphabetic,

The lists with all the favored.

Your persuasion acts upon me

Like a poisonous emetic.

You are too analytical.

You lack humor

And the human touch.

You push too far for Pyrrhic victories

Which bleed you.

(You are like the corpse at the door,

Knocking but ignored.)

My goods go with me, on the fire.

Besides, it is written, signed and attested to

By feed solicitors

Who understand the letter only,

Exacting its toll strictly.

Your face sickens, your palms sweat

And the room begins to quake.

Mostly, I disdain your company

On mountain tops.

There is not room enough.

You offer

What is not yours to give

Nor mine to take.

Your finger contaminates with pointing.

You stalk the room like a bridegroom at the wake.

Your presence, with its lingering,

Infects the air with a grave pestilence.

I am no Macbeth.

You are not his witches.

Though I wish his eloquence

I reject the blood of his ambition.   *1964*

Swarm of Smiling Bastards

I will repopulate the earth with a swarm of smiling
bastards

Who will move on Constantinople on the first clear
morning.

They will attack on tiptoe

And bomb the bridges in their fast-receding rear,

Out-maneuvering the Mickey Mouse militia

(Overcome with the singing of old school songs.)

I will reinstate the dignity of air,

The sun free rein, to the rising of.

And I will accept no apologies

From the humble licking pharisees,

Until my door they slide beneath,

Dated properly,

Their resignations irreversibly signed

And bequeath their estates to the bears,

To wander in the desert

And return with their heads in their hands.   *1964*

The Giant's Lost His Only Eye

I've made a pact

To arrange for the theft

Of the golden goose,

No mind of golden eggs

Delivered nightly

To the barred back door,

In devious propitiation

By the paper crated dozen.

I've laid in wait

Like a brat on Christmas Eve,

Beneath a tree,

To unbeard the chuckling rogue

For a merry tub of lard.

The giant's lost his only eye

And I've come back,

Nor notified the New York Times.

On the sly,

Behind my guide's turned back,

I've stashed photographs

In a safe place,

Until the proper time,

While I'm coming to terms

With the people from Life

For the right price.   *1965*

Sing the Numbers

Uncounted by the senseless census takers

Hiding in the dying trees,

I will sing the numbers

Down the darkening stairway to the street.

I will beat the drum on Cadillac roofs

And run jumping from roof to roof

On jammed freeways of lost desire.

I will sing the old chansons of yesteryear.

I will be here, stay here, enduring,

After all the Armageddons sign a truce

On paper,

On the decks of a Missouri

That will not sink.

I will sound the bugle in absentia

And will hand deliver souvenir pens

To the attending intelligentsia,

Embossed with my unembarrassed Logo,

My two-bit blurb.   *1967*

A Secret Affinity with Kilroy

I share a secret affinity with Kilroy

Who has yet to be clearly spotted

Switching the key letters.

I was once accused of using his name

But the case was dropped.

I went into hiding with the evidence

In my head.

I have been reported alive in Brazil,

Spotted,

By provocateurs on a side street in Portugal.

My meals arrive precooked.

I am wise and make no smoke.

I have friends on the outside

Who speak my name

And advise me to stay exactly where I am.

The story of my night wanderings

Will be kept by the uniformed Doorman

Who I never forget at Christmas.   *1966*

I Never Sold My Harvest Whole to Gallo

I have triumphed, to some degree,

In the cultivation

Of my own particular attributes.

I have harangued my detractors

In the street,

And herded them like sheep,

Danced to the music of their bleat.

I never sold my harvest whole

To Gallo.

Wine grapes from vineyards I brought from seed

Were plowed back to black

And thicken

My inorganic needs.

(I will darken rivers.)

I have champagned ships

Out into the sea,

For the self-esteem of sails

Big bellied against

The screw ship sooted sky.

I have hawked the ballast

On rivieras and jungle rivers,

An unmeltable heavy hail

(Shoveled from the streets,

Filling pushcarts)

Like cat's eye marbles

Glowing in the heat.

I have walked upon the beach

And made a serious offer,

Like a ruined capitalist.

My lost ships are coming in,

Escorted by a regatta

Of shrimp boats

Cheering madly for the wind;

From the orient

After decades

And I am beside myself with grief.   *1965*

Chalk Man

Cheated of the convenience of excuses,

Not to be able to say,

This, this is lacking

And nothing more.

This is the trick of the chalk man

Crippled with gifts

Who beat knuckles bloody on the door;

Santa Claus with ash in his fist

And booze on his breath;

A kin to that snickering Footman,

Lackey to the late John Beresford Tipton

And his damned carte blanche.

1966

My Camels Have Been Slaughtered

From the kings of unholy Christendom,

In exile, on pain of death,

Proclaimed usurper and malcontent,

I journeyed to the court

Of the Emperor of China,

Never once looking back.

There were no banners at the city gates,

Waving welcomes in the wind,

No palms to soothe my way.

Upon my arrival my beasts of burden

Were slaughtered ritualistically,

Exquisitely,

Politely returned to me

Served on porcelain platters,

As if an ancient, honored custom,

Denoting the extremest expression

Of the hospitality of their own ancestors,

Which they, perhaps, misunderstood,

Or misapplied,

Being ignorant of this particular beast.

They bow and smile,

As if I should kiss my fingertips

Wet with their delectable sauces.

My camels have been slaughtered

And I have become the talk

Of kitchen gourmets,

Fat, gouty and loquacious,

Obsequious in adulation

But entirely inconsequential.

1964

In the Name of My Father

The name of my father grew up with me

As if he were not dead.

I was filled by his presence,

As if a hand reached out from heaven,

And I, condemned, a lesser Michelangelo,

To set down the sentence,

Forever, with a chisel.

With my father's passing

An era ended.

The flowers did not smell so sweet,

The fruit fell too early from the bough,

People sickened and would not eat.

He reigned in a closed circle

Of displaced people

Yearning for repatriation.

Fortunate, his sphere knew few critics.

He was hated only by his enemies.

Ruthless in his expectations,

He ruined the lesser of his progeny

And they devoured him.

My mother lived only

In my father's memory.

She would have given half a life

To make him live.

There were no takers.

She spent his life's fortune in revenge,

Cultivating a fetish for crazy hats,

Boxes falling out of stuffed closets.

She took a second husband

In desperation,

And supported him,

Incapacitated satyr

To the stone-dead Hyperion.

After death, the family continued to exist,

In whispers,

Reciting the name, among themselves,

Like a secret, an incantation, long, Slavic,

And impossible to pronounce in English.   *1968*

Betsy

Betsy was the prettiest girl

Who hung by a thread to a bygone age

Where decked out beaus

In starched choked collars

Came parading by on tiptoe

Begging only the mercy

Of her smile.

Renaissance men sans gentleness,

With scissors of this century,

Mind reading sonneteers

Drew shivers.

She was schoolmarm stiff

In Woodstock's midst

And scrutinized the toll exacted of her

As if it were a Picasso,

Lines acid etched in mirror glass

For breakfast,

Her universe stirred from the bottom

Of demitasse cups,

A gift from her late mother,

Conceived herself

Manning walls against the onslaught,

Subsisting in the ruins,

Yearning for the security

Of a sexless sugar daddy

To bankroll a small boutique,

Slice her loose

Of the schoolroom's yoke,

Lascivious joke of horny adolescents.

Her dreams were infinitesimal.

Her mother married beneath her.

Her father, a diabetic double amputee,

Half illiterate, beloved brother,

Retarded.

Betsy had a mind made for doilies.

Hers was the merest quaint civility,

Which will yet be missed.   *1972*

Join the Natives

Once and for all,

I am waiting for the inside story;

To be awakened by a phone call

In the middle of the night,

A voice I know, but <u>can</u> <u>not</u> place.

Someone I sent out years ago,

To the other side, of the world, perhaps,

And somehow didn't expect to come back,

But to change their name

Join the natives and eat boiled rice.

I stay awake to hear

The back porch creak

And know it isn't thieves.

I've affixed my name

To a legal sounding sheet

Under extreme duress,

And exist only by stealth

Continuing to elude the universal call up.   *1965*

The Fisherman and Politicians

Diluvian sprites sing secular hymns

And spook the night.

They are silent lying

In the tall grasses of the salt marshes,

To hook a poet rafted,

Oarless with unplugged ears,

To occupy his mind

With their song's memorization,

And to spill it

Like his held in guts

Brutally down stream

To the fisherman and politicians.

1963

Bleeding in the Night

Once, when they were young,

In solemn parade, they carried,

With dignified pomp, on their shoulders high,

Like a fallen warrior angel,

The bravest of their comrades, sleeping,

And left him alone locked in a haunted house,

As a kind of practical joke, I guess,

While they all listened, hidden in the attic,

Closets, behind the couch.

He awoke as if born to the spot,

Looked about, tried the doors,

Jimmied a window and climbed out.

Left behind without him

It was they who became afraid.

His ingenuity was enviable

And amazed them.

Which one of them

Would not have stumbled about,

Pounded doors impotently

At the top of their voice

Or gone crashing through the glass

To lay bleeding in the night.

1964

Anthems to the End

We seek catharsis,

Beat drums to purge our mist,

Cheer lead the accompaniment

To drown the blood beat.

Fractured fingers fine tune

The lunatics exegesis.

Ears stick to antiques.

A cracked victor speaker holds forth

Scratching needles into flesh,

Which craves transfusion and inclusion.

Fear no flying objects.

Stone deaf,

We sing all anthems to the end

Still standing.

Warned in advance,

We exit before the blood bath.   *1962*

Spasm of Wasted Heat

We are only mocked by a final wakefulness

Which, too late, accuses us of sleep.

It is this inconvenient waking, only,

Which makes the judgment so.

We have jumped in youth,

Grown used to a universe of rushing air,

Forced within our nostrils,

Arms flung futilely

To pick a pin's dot

And triumphantly repeat,

There, there is where I'll land;

To flap our hands

In a spasm of wasted heat,

Our eyes, wide,

Finally,

To see the land, arise,

Divide,

And close again.   *1962*

I Have Searched

I have searched millennia.

God, I have searched

For blue skies, green fields

Ground solid under feet,

Woods to walk in, seas you could swim in,

A sun to bask in, a body to laugh in.

But this is all,

All some fool trick,

Not at all,

At all as I would have imagined it,

Like I dreamed it, wished for it,

Or would have created it.

The natives speak in tongues,

A mean patois approaching gibberish.

Wise men are buried underfoot,

While mountebanks reign like roosters

Cakewalking in the sun

But deadly serious.

Murderous morons broken loose

Crack the treasury in the street,

The king's chest split

Like a watermelon hatcheted,

Goons all gussied up

And jewel bedecked,

Flaunting gauds,

Like savages in top hats

From the envoys they ate,

Ear to ear grins, picking teeth,

Gluttonous, slothful, profligate,

They stink from meat,

Spawn like vermin in the grain bin.   *1964*

Prophets

The age of prophets is over.

The head upon the platter

Is busy greeting guests

And sings accompaniment to the dancers

Upon request.

We crucify our saviors in the cradle,

Encourage carnivorous cows

To devour them in mangers.

Golgothas are inconvenient

In an age of anesthesia.

Butchery is superseded

By the sterile solution

Of bloodless lobotomies.

Torturers are succeeded by technicians

Especially adept

At personality disorders

And diseases of the brain.

King Herod and his merry men

Enthrone themselves,

Behind desks of painted steel,

Push papers

Which make men bleed.   *1963*

The Track

Fanatics come to scream,

No blood bleed.

A wholly secular vision balloons their desire,

A score of winos run for the one muscatel.

The bookie pimp is one mean handicapper,

Broken limbs inflicts with excruciating logic.

Kneeling at the rail for a rationing of crutch,

The dole is apportioned in pleated paper cups,

Shot glasses fist crushed.

They file up to the window,

Bare-assed for the fix,

Rocking arms will hold them tight

Like Mama's,

For one more revolution

Of earth

In space.   *1963*

Compose yourself.

Compose yourself.

Ringing ears concoct a music

From the shell shock experience has left.

We unstick;

Bereft, retract our secret missives.

Knowledge intellectualized anesthetizes.

Sages withstand, intact,

Sitting fat wise,

Glazed Buddhas abnegating

The unkeepable prize,

Sandbagged against onslaughts of time.

The mind gluts upon itself,

Caponed cleric,

Monking time away

In middle age monasteries of inertia.   *1964*

Armadas in the Sun

I dream of anarchic indolence.

I lose my ease in the presence of mine enemies.

I bid good riddance to the valiant violence

Of my youth.

I am pursuing my commission,

The command of wooden porches,

Armadas in the sun.

1962

Encoded In Eden

I sink into exaltations, easy and gentle,

As if into my grandfather's greatcoat,

Birth given, to ward off world chill,

Armor to storm any hill with.

Slit loose from the blooded cells

Of warming silence

My logic incises and appalls.

Ill at ease, here, among these legions,

My genes were encoded in Eden.

Expectations are excessive and ensnare.

The acquired infection

Could not be blood transmitted.

We, each, reenact a travesty of falling.

Prosperous citizens, trigger fingers cocked,

Eye us, the aliens, wary of the prey.

If we are victors, how then do we differ?

We have adopted their devises

And adapted we endure.

I sink into exaltations as if into an Eden

Encoded in my genes.

I sleep into elations,

Lock up my cutting logic

And rock shut my eyes.   *1965*

The King Is Dead

A horseman carries heavy tidings

And a price upon his head.

The king is dead,

The king is dead,

And they have named a mountebank

To reign triumphant in his stead.

He lays his head among the daisies of the field

And leaves his horse to roam among the green.

He meets the fairest maid he has ever seen.

Messengers here are stricken down

For what messages they bear.

These beings here, quaint and cunning,

Disembowel their disturbers.

Let them sleep in slovenly peace.

The grass is green

And the wind is alive and galloping in the trees

And the young pretty girls are winsome

And believe.   *1965*

The Primal Chief

Venturing into the interior,

I have met the primal chief

With pointed smiling teeth,

Wearing the high silk hat

Which once smartly bedecked

My dearly departed brother,

Who preceded me.

1964

The Ex-President

"I try to begin again,

Move to resume my former stance,

High up, at the speaker's podium.

I attempt to climb the temporary scaffolding

And I am pulled aside,

To my knees, not recognized.

I produce identifying credentials.

Quickly shifting eyes survey my profile,

Compare me to the photograph

They handle,

Issued by the high authorities

For veneration,

Marred for preservation

In transparent plastic.

They did not expect me in the flesh.

They tell me I've grown old,

My voice grown cracked,

It would not be well for me

That I should speak

To blemish the well-remembered resonance

Of my former voice.

The words no one remembers.

They want no spectacle,

Nor wish they to embarrass me.

They will relay the regards of the ex-president.

They promise,

Then they lead me back,

Down the stairs.

They will make no martyr of me,

Not hang me to a multitude of jeering people.

The scaffolding is saved for speeches now.

The deeds that were begun by me

Cease to be my deeds.

Quietly I will be buried

Praised by my betrayers.

They will blast my argumentative epitaph

In rock

And sing my benedictions, basso profundo,

From the altar rail with gusto."   *1966*

A Tomb Becomes My Taj Mahal

Claws are cut when lions young,

Clumsy stubs run with blood,

With murals streak the dungeon cell,

A piece of earth exudes the fatal smell,

A tomb becomes a Taj Mahal.

Catapulted in ascendancies of fire,

A meteoric kite rains a red rust ash.

Raise an orchestrated babel

To a land of sky silent giants.

Recite Fo Fum.

Against the night crazy patterns reappear,

Footprints in the blood

Tracked across the rising of the sun.

1966

All My Names

I load my mules with worthless baubles

Captured from the sky

To bribe the warring brides of the abyss,

But they have diamonds in their eyes

And already

They know all my names

And why I have arrived.

1966

A Pocket Full of Kernels

A pocket full of kernels flung indifferently.

Upon the sober morrow

Arise yesterday's sleeping monsters,

Groveling in the inklings

Of incipient animation,

Sprung from the falling teeth

Littering the retreating path

Of beaten dragons spitting flint.

1962

Pale Men

This is the age of sophistication.

The warriors have designated

No successors,

Nor forwarding addresses

And left no bequests.

I am besieged by pale men

With white flour puffed on plump faces

Over armed with brief cases.

1965

Fish Monger

A fishmonger turned importer serves

A sorceror's apprenticeship in

Broken Latin.

He has grown unusually prolific,

Big as a circus baloon

Racing up the sky

With big boots on.

Enormous dreams gone sour,

Yeastily amoebic,

Are rising in the dark,

Come to nudge him as he dozes,

To tug at him

Like some reluctant shy lover

Whom he deserted,

To take him on a romp

In remembrance,

To drag him by the hair

Through the middle of the night.   *1963*

The Bull

The bull alone encompasses

The field he stands in,

Creating himself the sun of any universe

He wanders in.

Proprietary preoccupations alien,

Unencumbered, unthreatened, unenthralled,

Landlord medievally casting eyes

Above the bounds of acquisitiveness.

Certain, secure, sanctified,

Pervading his own being

With a grandeur of himself,

Integrated, unannexed,

Himself his own too solid flesh.

He exudes it,

Yearning after no exegeses,

No esoteric dialectic to debilitate

His overwhelming presence,

Autonomous,

Physicality beyond the pettiness of egotism,

Opposite to the gossiping cud sedated cows,

Soiled by the easy palm of sociability.

Kingly,

But unkin to the degenerate inbred aristocracies

Europe stooped to.

Kingly,

Like the old dead absolute kings

Of story book magnanimity.

1965

The Indo-Chinese Catfish

Disgust,

In the indolence of tolerated ineptitude,

The Atlantic conspires to join the Pacific

In league with the upland lakes,

The fish of which have begun to leave

By the quickest means.

The Indo-Chinese catfish

Have taken to the thoroughfares

Scattering the house broken Siamese cats.

1966

Whales Alive

I am waiting for the time

When chickens learn to fly

And hover above the chimney tops

In gigantic singing flocks,

Sooted black against a yellow sky,

When the giants will be freed

And not condemned for their giantry.

I am waiting for the time

When retired brigadiers

Will laugh in broken tears,

When the mariners will take up sides

And bring back talking whales

Alive.

1968

Shoe-less Landlord

Scribbling with a maniac's magnificence

On a gas station map

With a magic marker,

Trying to trace the crossroads back

To where the dreams were lost,

Like suitcases tossed

From tenement windows,

To elude the shoe-less landlord

Hiding in the bushes.

And if he had caught you,

What could he have done,

Arrested you?

Dot a coloring book landscape

With red topped pins,

Blood pricks to indicate

Your forgotten sins.

1961

Foreign Language

I learned this foreign language

To teach the foreigners mine,

Fluently powerless,

I cannot remember my original tongue.

By the time that they were mine

I was also theirs.

Late at night

When all the house is asleep,

Steeped in its own,

As if inebriated, sumptuousness,

I attempt a syllable or two

Before a mirror.

The movement of the lips distracts me.

If I could hear it from another,

Only once, I think it would all come back.

I wonder if from where I came

Still exists, <u>any</u> <u>where</u>, except in me.   *1961*

Mapless Magi Through the Rye

Swim skin deep in the Olympian surface

Of these things.

An incognito king moves

Amongst a subject people

Like a captured god

Exchanging pleasantries and knowing winks,

With a stern and steadfast duty

To devirginate

Every golden girl of beauty,

Who, lost angels of an alien god,

Dance like mapless magi

Through the rye.

1961

The Sky Writer's Autograph

The sky writer's autograph

Purposely cryptic,

Can easily be interpreted as obscene,

Castrated by the ass kissing clowns

Of chaos

Wielding sharpened shears.

The word is diluted by the winds inroads.

Cut down the leaders.

To initiate the slaughter

Spill the boldest blood.

Oblivion creeps

Like an infectious disease.

Bubonic plague consumes

A colony of lepers.

A dull stick etches sand

In a windy desert.   *1961*

Cheer Me, Marco Polo

I clutch for souvenirs, tightly,

As if my life,

Mementos of my Odyssey.

Tediously I am dragged

In a rain drenched cloak

Which weighs me heavily in the flood.

A momentary visit seemed a life.

I clench my fists upon twisting twigs,

Bleeding blisters on my palms

Will testify,

The knife wound in my side.

I will tear the raveling hair

And hold on tight.

They will cheer me, Marco Polo,

Through a corridor of shoulders

And question me of the alleged existence

Of an Atlantis in the sea.

I will return with gold doubloons

And pour dunes of sand

From my dream worn shoes.   1962

Shattered Glass

Words are spun,

Blown glass brimmed

With sipped champagne,

Faltering in the crystal atmosphere.

My toast is dizzying me

Toward the edge of a ravine

Of my release,

Which finds its music in the crash,

Delirious laugh,

One by one,

The fireplace is littered

With my shattered glass,

To which my guests will testify,

Shoes forgotten

In the numbness of their bleeding feet.

1962

Come Back Lazarus

Have I friends beyond this speck?

Have they sent me,

Ignorant emissary,

Who forgets his message

On the way,

As a kind of cosmic joke,

To retrieves the sweetest mysteries

Of a hell

We, otherwise, could never know?

Will I come back Lazarus

From the jaws of death

With daisy crowns upon my head?

1962

Manna

The longer that I sit

The more I will find fault

With all of it.

I have made a game of it.

Upon me soon will be the winter famine

And still I will not eat.

Solemnly,

In the beginning of the falling snow

I sit

And nothing will be done for this.

I wait for manna from the heavens

And I starve to death.

1962

Swaggers Death

Razor keen and eager,

Kicks the dust and spits,

Swaggers death forth, inebriate,

Insomniac, screwed to the task,

Unknotting knots we pulled so tight

With such deliberate concentration

And devotion.

1965

Garden Dream

One could grow accustomed

To a labyrinth of inconsistencies,

As if shaken

From a sunny garden dream,

Unconcernedly lapsed into,

In the lulling midst

Of the humming security

Of talking friends,

Talking somewhere still.

Reconstituted ignorantly

Into some far-flung corner

Of an unheard of universe,

Pinned beneath the matter

Of foreign contingencies,

Heaped upon me

Like monuments of victory.

I suspect

I have not graduated

To a higher form of flesh.   *1964*

Solutions

"If as an animal I must die,

My blood I will spit into my captor's eye.

My arms will fly,

If severed, yet into their face.

I will beat them with my fleshless bones,

Until my bones break.

I will cry and scream the name.

The carnage will be known,

The blood seen,

And none will dare to call it

By any other name.

And the words will choke in their throats

From the stench of my rotting blood:

My spattered guts

Broadcast across their public edifices

Will stain indelibly

And no one,

No one will forget."   *1966*

Illiterate in Precepts

I am illiterate in precepts

Even these.

Granted time

I could utter wise cracks

To an unhearing universe,

Ambassadors dispatched,

Over-dressed, diplomatic dry wits,

Inept in the mechanics,

First in the lists,

Proceeding unrepentant.   *1967*

Tipping of a Hat

When the sun begins to run,

When at its height its dying rays

Descend as red as ill-gotten luck,

No more matter than the final,

Gallant,

Tipping of a hat,

Remember,

Clutching at the crack,

Of every new born day,

Settling into cozy complacencies,

And obscene inevitabilities.

You salaried your soul away,

Accepting intact,

The hard bound book

Of settled, safe, transportable fact.

You were poured like melted wax.   *1962*

Rome Was More Conquered

Strict and enforceable laws

Of inheritance exist.

Beware of solicitors

Bearing blank checks,

Of unexpected legacies

Propped against unopened doors.

The deaths of anonymous dowager aunts

Have clauses full of cats,

Which scratch,

Closets full of curios chock full far

Of invisible, influential,

Administrative Greeks.

Rome was more conquered than

Greece could be.

Though born in the East

I was reared in the West.

I am a fine judge of horse flesh

And look all my gifts quickly

In the mouth

For rotten teeth and contagious

Gum disease.

1967

Gambler

I set my pace

By the betting men who dog my trail,

Buying up my discounted debts.

One night I will get out,

Through the cracked skylight

In the roof,

Which home runs,

Batted from the park broke.

1962

Far Louder Than Goliath

In the alley rear of our lives,

Tin cans strewn, littering our minds,

Walking on our ears we hear

Footfalls louder than our own two feet

Could ever beat.

We will be pressed in our own stampede.

We suspect, we skip a step

And listen twice.

Around we wheel on one sharp heel,

Indignantly, strike a cocky posture,

Anachronistically absurd.

The nineteenth century

Would give a hearty cheer.

Chin pointing pugilist will call a dare

Far louder than Goliath would

Stripped to the armor of his hair.   *1967*

Make a List

Make a list of the brawny and big.

Snap the whip, standing in the sun,

Whispering, call them near.

Nod the high sign, for them to begin.

Plunge the dipper down to crowded cheers

Wild with expectations of belief,

Lunge out broadly in the street

Smiling signed invitations.

Fill your fists with flowering weeds

Plucked from cracks in the concrete.

1962

Vibrations

When within,

When at peace,

Drugged asleep

By an after dinner drink,

Be reminded of the war

That wages in the street,

By the vibrations

Of distant destruction

Raising an objection.

1964

Crucifixion

I marvel at the often bizarre but beautiful scaffoldings
that men erect to bedeck themselves, to hold
themselves up and intact, to give structure where
there is none, to fortify and stretch out the remnants
of their collapsed ruins. We are men of straw who hang
ourselves, like worn old clothes on dilapidated crosses
of castoff, broken wood which cannot hope to hold
even our own weight, who even the crows violate; but
do not tell me this is an unworthy crucifixion. A man
stuck on a cross, especially, with focused wits which
crucifixion will assuredly concentrate, should not
waste his time dispensing platitudes.

2015

Jackie Gleason

I had an uncle, a man I had great affection for, who did a dead on imitation of Jackie Gleason, an imitation which was his life. He spoke like Gleason; he was Jackie Gleason. He ate too much; he drank too much; he was a raconteur; he was immensely lovable and he was smart and funny. Now the question is: was he like that prior to his absorbed consciousness of Gleason or was Gleason himself tying in to a whole set of values and mannerisms that preexisted, out there, in the social ether and did they both tap in to common roots? There was something quintessentially Irish about Gleason. My uncle was christened Michael but called himself Mickey, a very Irish moniker. When tanked-up he titled himself an Old Russian, which was closer to the truth, technically; certainly he had the muzhik about him. He was Leonid Brezhnev, Richard Daley, Arthur Kroc; but most of all, most certainly, he was purposefully and admiringly Jackie Gleason, the one and only; he owned every single one of his records. No, there is no doubt about it; he reinvented himself modeled against a person that he never met, that very well may not have existed, did not, in fact, exist; a creation of the performer, the image he projected; Gleason himself was never so sweet in real life, and this artificial sweetness no doubt sweetened the man my uncle might otherwise have been, that he absorbed only via an insubstantial, glittering display of flickering artificial light from a cathode ray vacuum tube. Why not Clark Gable or Cary Grant? Out of his league. In Gleason, along with the immeasurable common man charm, he could indulge the other person he himself had been, a legitimization of his gross fallibility, an easy dispensation for his most conspicuous lapses: alcoholic, gluttonous and a bit of the buffoon but a genuine character as real as rain. It granted him absolution to descend when uncontrollably, miserably drunk into Ralph Kramden, a vulgar, crude, ignorant blowhard.

But who is to say the best man is not the man of the tube; that the TV persona was not the real Jackie Gleason; his best foot forward, the man most acceptable, the man he wished and hoped to be on his best day in the best possible world.

Was my uncle real? Was this an imitation of an imitation, an act based upon an act, a submergence of identity into some nebulous mass culture or were his sources rather an ever expanding birthplace and birthright, of far richer possibility of self-realization, of deeper wells magnified and multiplied, supplying a fertile cornucopia to critically and carefully choose from? There is a mass culture that enriches and enlarges us and a mass culture that degrades and demeans us. The all-pervading modern media, the great corrupter and destroyer of societal values, also facilitates a process of class simulation and emulation; and lets us impersonate giants who blow themselves up in our faces.

2015

John Marks

There was a consummate salesman who shattered all records. John Marks, a cold, hard man to his peers, stingy with his smiles and grudging of a word, kind or otherwise. But when a "customer" walked in he came to life like a dead man rising from the anesthetizing table, resurrected; he lit up the sky like the Fourth of July. His smile could mesmerize a concert hall and bring the congregation stomping to its feet. He was loved by his customers; they were his friends, perhaps his truest friends, his only friends. Who is to say that this fabulation, this construct, this paradigm was not the real John Marks; the man he would be in a kinder, gentler world of his craftily secreted dreams ... the best of all worlds; the ultimate reality of the celebrated actor stumbling off the real stage into his accustomed protective coma. A successful salesman requires a rhinoceros's hide; but there is a kind of immunity on whatever stage; bombarded with whistles and boos, catcalls and hoots, it is all a piece with the charade; remove the bloody wounds with a costume change; nothing ventured, nothing risked, your core inviolable; the purported mask is armor plate of Damascene steel.

Life is on the boards or in the magician's Chinese regalia, its inscrutable make-up, or on the tight rope or the flying trapeze; the conjuror before his audience comes to life; everything else is anticipation or anticlimax. What did Wallenda say?

> "Being on a tightrope is living; everything else is waiting."

2015

Petersen

I knew a fellow who repeated a story that was genuinely touching. His name was Peterson and he spoke of his Norwegian mother with an almost holy reverence.

Peterson:

> "I remember every Saturday night Mama would sit down at the kitchen table and count out the money Papa had brought home in his pay envelope.
>
> "She would carefully count out various stacks.
>
> "'First of all for the landlord' Mama would say, separating out the money.
>
> "'Second, for the grocer.' And yet another pile.
>
> "'For John's shoes.' That was my older brother, John.
>
> And we would all watch in fear as the original pile got smaller and smaller.
>
> At last Papa would ask: 'Is that all?'
>
> And Mama would nod and finally we could breathe easy.
>
> Mama would look up and smile at each of us in turn. 'It is good,' she'd say. 'We have enough' ".

Peterson never tired of telling this story, endless times, like a ritual incantation, a founding, sustaining myth, varying only slightly each time. Tears would well up in his eyes and I was always moved, somewhat. It always sounded unsettlingly familiar, like I had heard it before somewhere, in a dream maybe; that it was unoriginal, a borrowed suit that doesn't fit right, big in the shoulders, too long in the sleeves; it rang false. One time when Peterson was performing his ceremonial with particular animation, his drinking buddy Joe, a prototypical Irishman, is standing in the background out of view of Peterson, making mugs, extravagant faces and an exaggerated jerk-off motion, howling in pantomime. I didn't have the heart to break up Peterson's accustomed routine, which seemed to mean a lot to him. But the next time I saw Joe I asked:

"What the hell was that all about?"

Joe:

"I'm tired a hearing that crock a shit. I heard it a thousand times. His mother wasn't Norwegian... his father was... so he says... or thinks. His mother was a drunken Irish whore who never paid a goddamn bill in her fucking life... stole every cent the poor old man brought home... snuck out and got drunk on it... that's why the father took off when Bob was a kid... went out one night when he found her drunk in her own vomit... whacked out on the floor and never came home again. And what's this Mama and Papa shit? Every other time it's 'my old man' or 'my old lady'.

Peterson was very proud of his Norwegian roots, of the father who wasn't there and never tired of telling people, who for some reason refused to believe he was Norwegian. He looked just like the Russian general who traded insults and toasted with Patton in the movie or maybe the actor who played the general. Everyone called him a Polack, friendly-like; strangers always speaking Polish to him like a compatriot, a brother. He even learned a few Polish words so he could fake it and be friendly back. But he hated the Poles and hated even more being taken for one:

"No, I'm Norwegian... really."

"Yeah... sure. I'm a fucking Eskimo. Who you tryin' to kid... kid?"

It is only later that I came to realize that the story he repeated so often was lifted almost verbatim from a tear-jerking movie I had watched as a kid; the heart-warming schmaltz: *I Remember Mama*. This was curious because Peterson was a tough guy who would fight anybody, no matter how big, who looked funny at him in any bar. I think if anybody told Peterson he was parroting back a movie script and quoted it back to him he would be dumbstruck, wouldn't know what to think, might unravel right there and lose his grip; this was part of the fantasy that allowed him to exist, the sustaining myth. What do you say or do when your exact double walks into the room and claims to be you?

Peterson was intelligent and very funny, missed his calling as a stage comedian, aced the Fire Captain's test, first in his precinct, an alcoholic who got falling down drunk in a bar every night of his life, but prided himself excessively for showing up every morning for work without fail. He was always running into fires, rescuing people. They gave him his own firehouse; made him Chief but took it away almost instantly when they caught him in the act, in flagrante delicto, getting a blowjob from some bimbo in his captain's car while "on duty" outside his firehouse; he was turned in by his own men who called him a "self-hating Negro" to his face, which totally stumped him. To his last day at his own House he had absolutely no idea what they were talking about.

2015

Paul Tripp

I had a friend who seemed especially broken up about a death one day. There were tears welling in his eyes. He was a man of fifty-seven not accustomed to tears. The year was 2002.

I remember asking:

"Was he a relative?"

Friend:

"No... until today I didn't even know his name. But it's opened up a flood of memories, like an iron gate rusted shut finally breaking open off the hinges.

"I saw his obituary in the New York Times and recognized the photograph.

"His name... I discovered was Paul Tripp. He was ninety-one.

"This sounds incredibly stupid but if it weren't for this man whose name I didn't know a week ago I don't think I would be alive today. He introduced me to the human race and made me part of it... want to be part of it. He had this television show whose name I had forgotten until the death notice: Mr. I. Magination."

This friend, more forthcoming than he usually was, remarkably so in a frightening way, described an incredibly bleak childhood in which his mother and her brothers took turns terrorizing and slapping him around. His sister, who he never remembers having a conversation with, didn't even know she was alive, inured, comatose, the unthinking slave of the adults but equally their victim. The nuns and priests were vicious, sadistic. If he could have run away he would have at four or five, anything to get away, but there was nowhere to run to.

The early days of television in the late forties and early fifties were an astonishing time, he explained as if speaking about an ancient history he had lived through:

"My mother, a vicious, stupid woman who everyone regarded as kind and generous and who I would always regard as clinically insane, purchased the magic box in 1949, manufactured by Dumont, for the astronomical sum of $900, the only rational purchase she ever made in her entire life. The small apartment we lived in had a market rent of $50 a month in an apartment house which had been owned by her dead husband, my father, a man of some wealth. Before his death the family had associated with doctors, lawyers and self-made entrepreneurs but after my father's passing she slid inexorably back to a level which accepted her, which she felt more comfortable with, from which she had risen, but much, much deeper down now to a kind of human sewer sludge of assorted low life who preyed upon her, extracting from her the ever depleting remnants of her husband's hard sweated wealth. She eventually married an old decrepit piece of the sewer sludge and gave him all the first husband's money so she could pretend to everybody that the sewer sludge had his own money; trying to prove that he may have been sewer sludge but at least he was sewer sludge with money. She became a drunk, joining the sewer sludge in getting wasted every single night; she had finally found her soulmate, descended to her perfect gutter level; happy as a pig in shit; the delivery boys weren't safe with her; forever fingering her rosary, addicted to novenas which she travelled to and hooked on suspect priests.

My father's children by a previous wife, who had died first, were taken by their grandmother. My mother warned me about these numerous half siblings as if they were demon spawn who would kill me if given the chance, break my neck or even torture me. They were all idiots, she said, rattling off their low IQs, name and number, which she was privy to. I attributed this to her spiteful resentment of the dead first wife and discounted it accordingly. But when I sought them out later in life with open arms full of naïve smiling hope for extending my family, having been isolated and "protected" from them by my crazy mother during my vulnerable years, I found to my absolute astonishment that she was right and she was right about almost nothing else. And not only about them being idiots; they would have killed me, no doubt about it; her prescient paranoia saved my life; she saved my life. I would have gone out an upper story window or drowned in a lake, "a tragic accident".

If my father had lived I, most certainly, would have died, painfully. I was too smart for my own good, which one of them warned me. Who the hell did I think I was? Be careful what you wish for. Be careful about wanting to rewrite history, of wanting to alter what you think is a cruel fate. And what did these fiends tell me about him, my father, this progenitor polluting the world with his foul semen, letting loose a brood of hateful degenerate morons? I dreamed in a fevered dream that my mother poisoned my father, to save me, her only son, from his host of evil progeny, a strange dream considering her latter perfect union with the piece of sewer sludge. I had never met people who dripped such thick venom; the hatred was palpable, intense and unambiguous; these were people who would hunt down and kill anyone they perceived as putting on airs which was anyone at all superior to themselves. I could feel it like the beast's scorching breath, sulfuric acid burning through my back.

The building we lived in was an island whose inhabitants clung precariously to a striving lower middle class, trying desperately not to become contaminated by the sub-human scum which always threatened to overwhelm us from the adjacent, encroaching buildings and intruding mean streets. I always especially despised the writers and media hounds, the flacks, the schlockmeisters of schmaltz who romanticized and fictionalized this despicable social stratum... an inept, maladroit way of attacking the decadent rich sideways but in the process disarming and emasculating those of us who fought so mightily... so desperately hard for our very lives, our existences, to rise out of this sloshing cesspool with its vicious undertow. Even the so-called realistic writers romanticize this stratum creating a more palatable world entirely of their own creation. They don't misremember, they lived in the fantasy... they survived through the fantasy. Money has absolutely nothing to do with any of it. Give this trash, this detritus, money and they become trash with money... infinitely more dangerous.

"And so the genie's in the glass bottle; the magic box opened up the world to me, revealed to me that there were humans who walked the planet earth, putting their best foot forward no doubt, kind and intelligent... that I was not alone, that there were others like me or rather like what I might come to be, not just the monsters who held me captive in their lunacy... and if not for this miracle, this medium, this perfect confluence of time and technology, would have gobbled me up, sliced thin on stale moldy bread or reduced me to a crippled automaton. Early television saved my life or brought me to life.

"'Mr. I. Magination', I just read, was directed by Yul Brynner, another maestro ... it ran weekly on CBS TV from 1949 to 1952... the benevolent Pied Piper, Paul Tripp, the engineer in striped overalls at the helm of a toy railroad train, surrounded by young children... which passed through a magic tunnel to the land of imagination... he would tell stories from history and literature: Rip Van Winkle, the life of P. T. Barnum. Later, he performed magic tricks with the leading illusionists of the day.

"This was the unexpected captivating intrusion of what passed for high culture. The very high price of the tube insured its exclusivity, the niche market of wealthy urbanized patrons ... I was lucky to live right across from Manhattan... the signal emanating straight from the Empire State Building might as well have been a supernatural beam from a bundle of sacred stardust... live telecasts of Shakespeare and music from Carnegie Hall.

"'Studio One', 'Kraft Television Theater', 'Philco Playhouse', 'Playhouse Ninety'. They grabbed the best actors from the Broadway legitimate theater.

"We have grown accustomed to actors with marbles in their mouths mumbling inaudibly in high pitched nasally whines. But I will never forget the hallucinatory voices of Ed Herlihy and Ralph Bellamy. We seem to have forgotten what a potent and persuasive, perfectly tuned instrument the human speaking voice can be."

I wondered if his grief hadn't overtaken his common sense; he had suffered catastrophic financial reverses recently, destroyed by an only son who he loved more than anything who for irrational or sub-rational reasons plotted against his father and thereby himself, destroyed a substantial fortune which only he was heir to; having once been a rich man, now ruined, at least in his own mind; or if he wasn't having some kind of a complete breakdown, a psychological collapse, having nothing at all to do with, but precipitated by, the death of a man whose name he had long ago forgotten or never knew and whom he had never once met.

I reminded him very gingerly of the "boob tube's", (my purposeful expression), "I Love Lucy", "Uncle Miltie" and "Howdy Doody". A little taken aback he simply insisted unconvincingly that he didn't like or watch those shows. He seemed to have blocked them out. They didn't fit his picture, his holy picture, the icon on the wall of his once magnificent house, boarded up and abandoned now, crumbling into clouds of choking dust. And Herlihy, while granted had a magnificent compelling instrument; he exploited it to hawk fake cheese. Alexander Scourby similarly blessed recorded the entire Bible for the blind without pay.

2015

www.ingramcontent.com/pod-product-compliance
Lightning Source LLC
Chambersburg PA
CBHW060134260626
47160CB00005B/2104